AMAZING OCEAN LIFE

Dolphins

by Colleen Sexton

Kaleidoscope
Minneapolis, MN

Where the Quest for Discovery Begins

This edition first published in 2023 by Kaleidoscope Publishing, Inc.

Kaleidoscope Publishing, Inc.
6012 Blue Circle Drive
Minnetonka, MN 55343

Library of Congress Control Number
2022937337

ISBN
978-1-64519-559-7 (library bound)
978-1-64519-629-7 (ebook)

Table of Contents

Wave Jumpers

Dolphins play in the ocean waves. They jump into the air and land with a splash!

Dolphins swim like fish. But they are **mammals**.

The sea is home to 38 kinds of dolphins. The largest is the orca. It is bigger than a bus!

Where Do Dolphins Live?

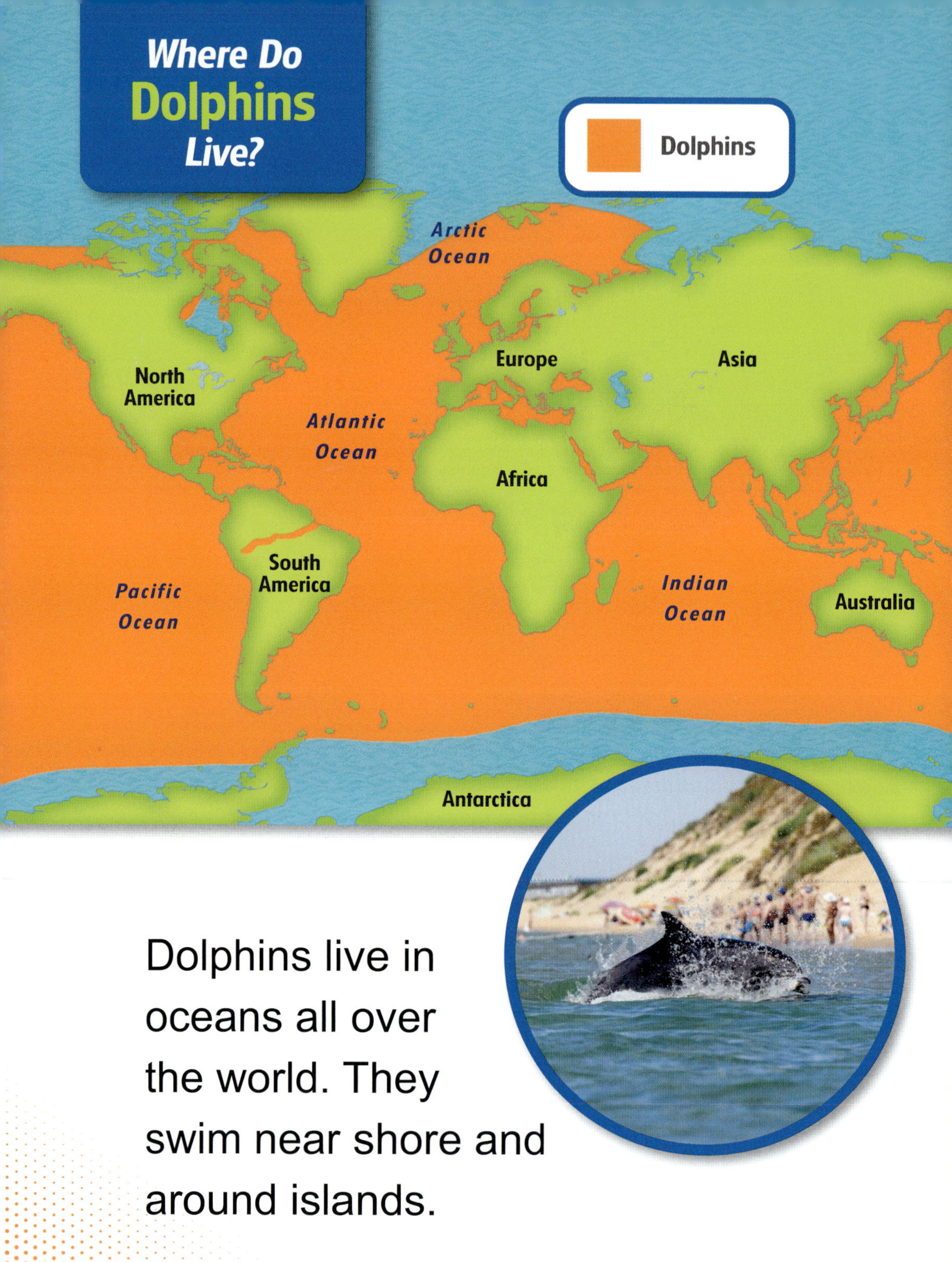

Dolphins live in oceans all over the world. They swim near shore and around islands.

They swim in open water, too. Dolphins can dive deep under the sea.

Built for Swimming

A dolphin has a long, curved body that is made for swimming. Smooth skin helps it slide through water.

A dolphin moves its two **flippers** to start, stop, and turn.

FUN FACT

Dolphins have big brains. They are among the smartest animals in the world.

A **dorsal fin** on its back keeps a dolphin from rolling over as it swims.

A dolphin jumps above the water to breathe air through a **blowhole**.

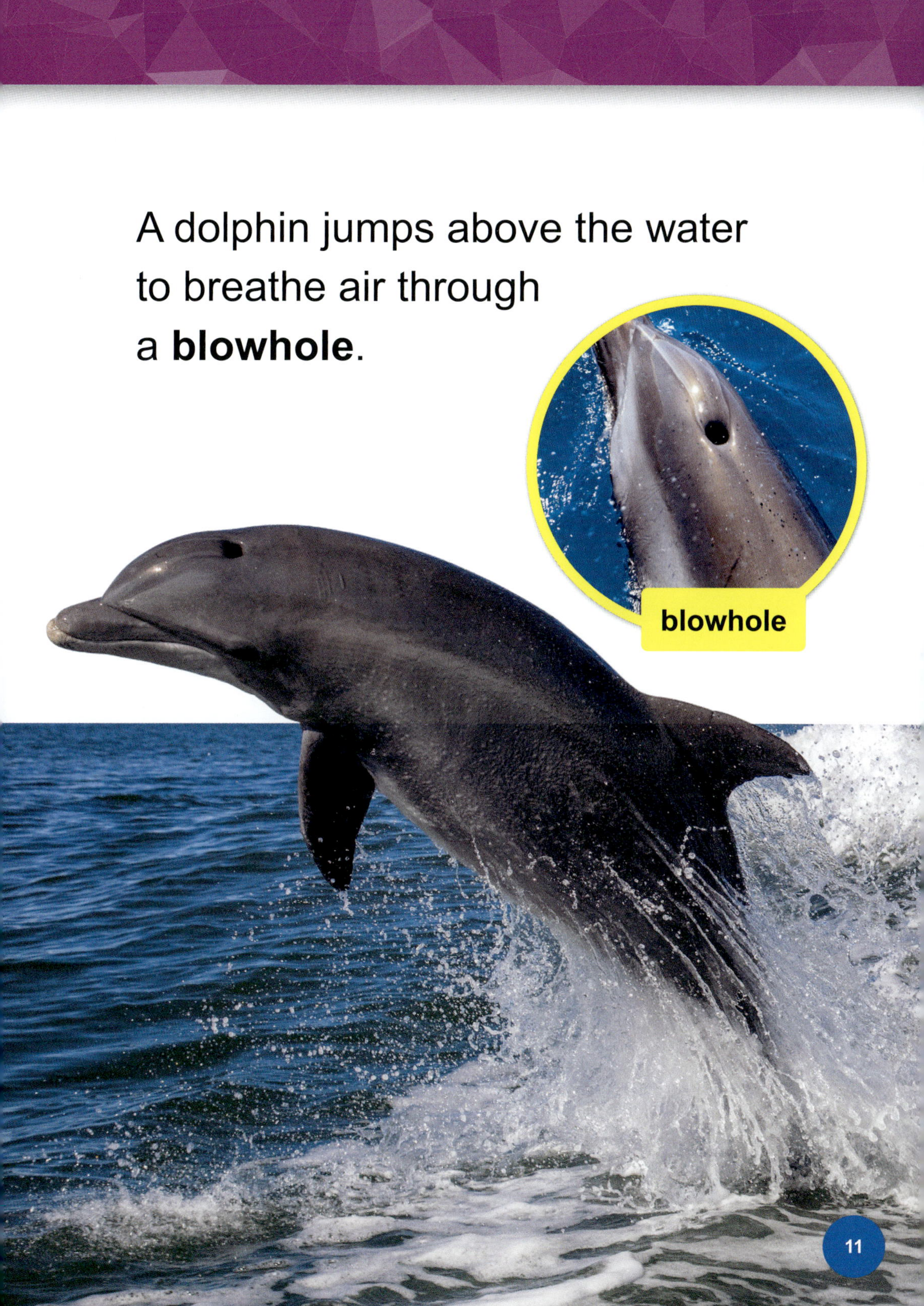

A dolphin's body ends in a tail. The tail has two big fins called **flukes**.

A dolphin moves its tail up and down to swim forward. Dolphins are speedy swimmers!

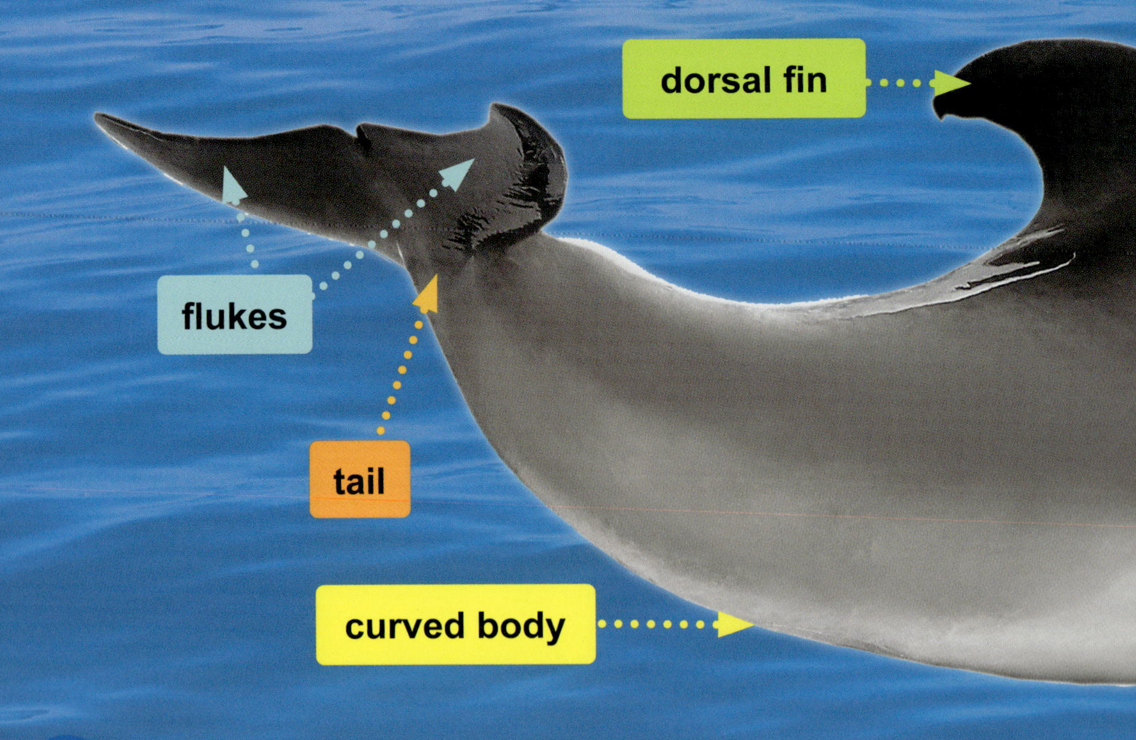

Parts of a Dolphin

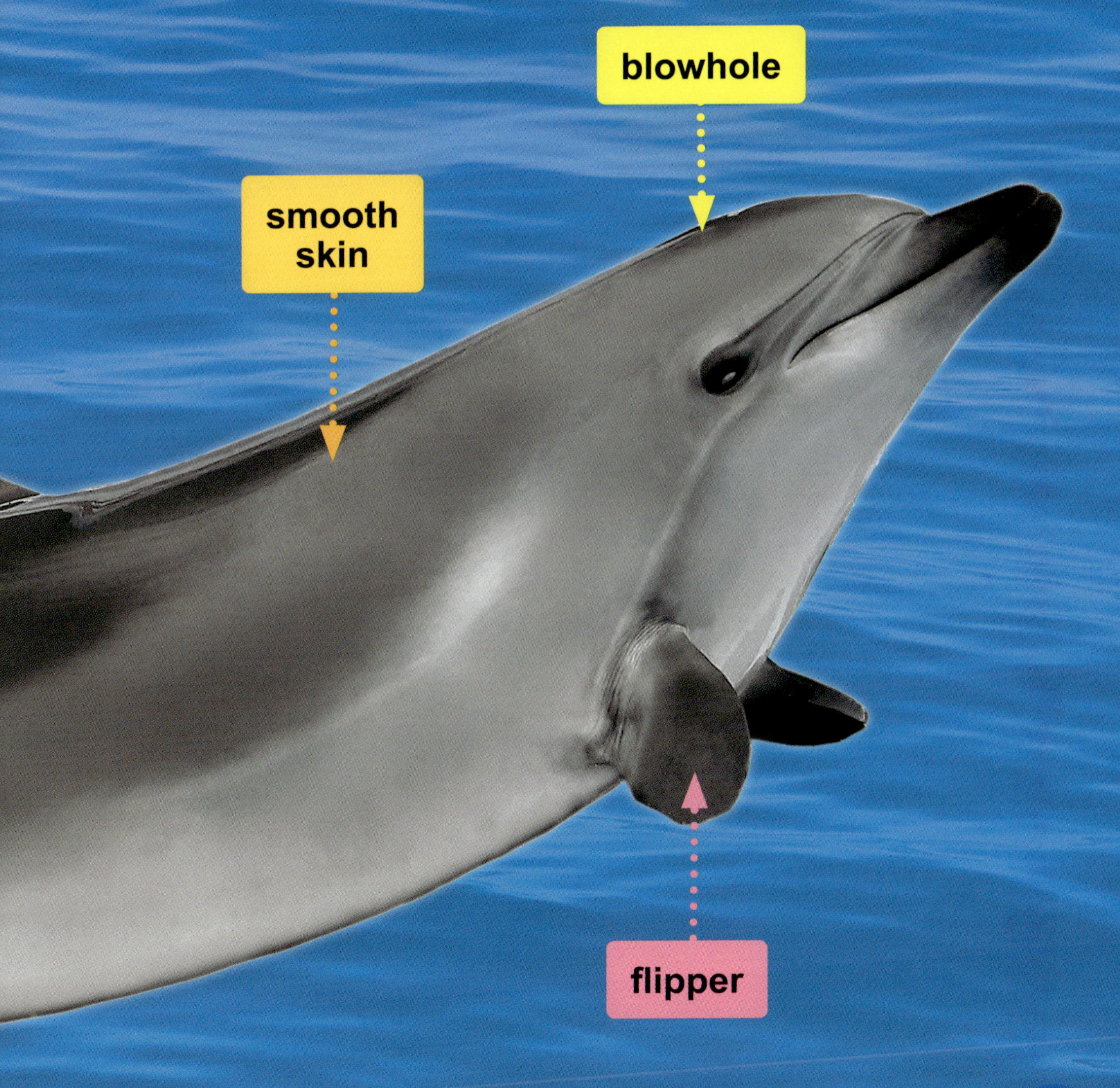

Pod Life

Dolphins live together in **pods**.
Some pods have a few dolphins.
Some have hundreds of dolphins.

The dolphins play together. They flip and spin in the air. They ride waves and blow bubbles.

Dolphins talk when they play and hunt. They warn each other when **predators** are near.

FUN FACT

Sometimes large dolphins eat small dolphins. But sharks are a dolphin's biggest predator.

The dolphins talk using many sounds. They make clicks, cries, squeaks, and other sounds.

On the Hunt

A dolphin hunts for food. The dolphin makes a clicking sound. The sound hits a fish and makes an **echo**.

The dolphin hears the echo. It tells the dolphin where the fish is. The dolphin chases the fish!

What do Dolphins Eat?

Sometimes dolphins team up. They swim around a big group of fish to gather them together.

A dolphin catches a fish with its sharp teeth. It swallows the fish in one gulp. Yum!

FUN FACT
Dolphins have pointed teeth. They are shaped like upside-down ice cream cones.

Photo Glossary

blowhole: A hole in the top of the head used for breathing. A dolphin jumps out of the water to breathe air through a blowhole.

dorsal fin: A fin on the backs of animals that live in the water. A dolphin's dorsal fin keeps it from rolling over as it swims.

echo: A sound repeats when it hits something. A dolphin hunts for food by making a clicking sound and listening for its echo.

flipper: A wide, flat arm-like part of sea animals used for swimming. A dolphin uses its two flippers to start, stop, and turn.

flukes: Flat fins on the tail of some sea creatures. A dolphin has two flukes on its tail.

mammals: Warm-blooded animals with hair or fur that usually give birth to live babies. Dolphins swim like a fish, but they are mammals.

pod: A group of one kind of sea animal living together. Dolphins live in pods.

predator: An animal that hunts other animals for food. Dolphins talk to warn each other when predators are near.

Read More

Mattern, Joanne. *Dolphins.* The World's Smartest Animals. Minneapolis, MN: Bellwether Media, 2021.

Schuh, Mari. *Dolphins*. The World of Ocean Animals. Minneapolis, MN: Jump!, 2022.

Zommer, Yuval. *The Big Book of the Blue.* New York, NY: Thames & Hudson, 2018.

Websites

Factsurfer.com gives you a safe, fun way to find more information.

1. Go to www.factsurfer.com.
2. Enter "Dolphins" into the search box and click 🔍
3. Select your book cover to see a list of related websites.

About the Author

Colleen Sexton is a writer and editor. She is the author of more than one hundred nonfiction books for kids on topics ranging from astronauts to glaciers to elephants. She lives in Minnesota.

INDEX

PHOTO CREDITS

The images in this book are reproduced through Shutterstock: Vincent Scherer 1, 23; SiiKA Photo 3; Liliya Butenko 4; Nerthuz 4; Willyam Bradberry 4-5, 16, 17, 22; Nikita Burdenkov 6; Andrea Izzotti 7, 18; Joost van Uffelen 8-9, 22; Gervasio S. _ Eureka_89 10; Dai Mar Tamarack 11, 22; Tory Kallman 11; photomaster 12-13, 22; bearacreative 14; New Africa 15; Nerthuz 16, 22; Halyna Parinova 19; IrinaK 19; Eric Isselee 19; bonchan 19; zhengzaishuru 19; SOMMAI 19; wildestanimal 20; Binson Calfort 21; Christian Musat 21; verca 21; Neirfy 22; Graeme Snow 22; optimarc 22; Jona Sanchez 22; Konstantin Novikov 22. Cover: Andrea Izzotti, Willyam Bradberry, Solarisys.